ms. Meane

CARTOON NETWORK

by E. S. Mooney
Based on
"THE POWERPUFF GIRLS,"
as created by Craig McCracken

SCHOLASTIC INC.

New York   Toronto   London   Auckland   Sydney
Mexico City   New Delhi   Hong Kong   Buenos Aires

ISBN 0-439-33213-3

Copyright © 2002 by Cartoon Network.
CARTOON NETWORK, the logo, THE POWERPUFF GIRLS, and all related characters and elements are trademarks of and © Cartoon Network. (s02)
Published by Scholastic Inc. All rights reserved.
SCHOLASTIC and associated logos are trademarks and/ or registered trademarks of Scholastic Inc.
Cover and interior illustrations by The Thompson Brothers

Designed by Peter Koblish

12 11 10 9 8 7 6 5 4 3 2 1   2 3 4 5 6 7/0

Printed in the U.S.A.
First Scholastic printing, April 2002

The city of Townsville! A happy city! A healthy city! A city that eats from the five basic food groups. . . . A city that likes its superheroes to be healthy, too!

The sun was just shining through The Powerpuff Girls' round bedroom windows. The Girls' alarm clock began to beep.

Blossom sat up in bed immediately. "Time to get up!"

Bubbles stretched and smiled. "Good morning, everybody!"

Buttercup smashed the beeping alarm clock. "Shut up!" she yelled at it.

Professor Utonium stuck his head in through the door. "Good morning, Girls," he said. "Time to get ready. I made an appointment for the three of you to have your yearly checkup this morning."

"But what about school?" Bubbles asked.

"Ah, we can skip school today," Buttercup said.

"You can go into school late today," the Professor said. "I've written Ms. Keane a note."

Later that morning!

The Girls hovered over the Professor's head as he walked up the path that led to the entrance of the Townsville University Physics and Aeronautics Laboratory. The Girls always had their checkups at the lab. An ordinary doctor never would have been able to test and check all their special superpowers.

"May I help you?" the woman at the desk asked.

"Yes, we have a nine-thirty appointment," the Professor explained.

"Certainly," the woman replied. "Have a seat, please."

The Girls and the Professor sat in the waiting room and looked at magazines. After a few minutes, a man and a woman, both dressed in white lab coats, came in.

"Girls, you remember Dr. Wick and Dr. Cratson from last year," the Professor said.

"Come this way, Girls," said Dr. Cratson.

The Girls and the Professor followed the two scientists into a large laboratory. All around them, scientists were working on different projects.

Blossom leaned over the shoulder of a

scientist who was scribbling away at some long math equations. "Excuse me," she said, "but I think you added there when you should have subtracted. The correct answer should be 67,987,456,333,234."

The scientist looked up at Blossom. "Oh, yes, you're right. Why, thank you."

Dr. Cratson chuckled. "Smart as ever, I see, Blossom," he said. "Now, I'm going to give you a hearing test." Dr. Cratson put some earphones on her head. "Listen carefully. Can you hear anything?"

Blossom nodded. "I can hear a beeping sound on the left side," she reported.

"Very good," Dr. Cratson said.

"And I can hear a little bit of static on the right," Blossom continued. "You may need to adjust the calibration of your earphones a bit."

"Oh," said Dr. Cratson, looking star-
tled.

"And I can hear a guy in the back
row of desks over there,"
Blossom went on. "He's
sniffing a little when he's
breathing — he may be
coming down with a cold
or something. And there's
a car outside over on Main
Street that has a little rattle
in its engine. And —"

"Okay, that's fine, Blossom," Dr. Cratson said, chuckling again. "Supersonic
hearing, check."

Dr. Wick led Bubbles toward a line
painted on the floor. "Now, Bubbles, just
stand on this line and look ahead of you at
that eye chart," she said. "Start at the top

and read out all the letters that you see."

Bubbles started reading the biggest letters at the top of the chart. "E — ooh, that's a nice letter. It stands for 'elephant,' a cute little elephant with big, floppy ears. Okay, the next letter is M. Oh, M for 'monkey'! The little monkey can ride on the elephant. And the next letter is H — that's for 'hats . . . .' "

Bubbles went on until she got to the tiniest letters at the bottom of the chart. She focused on the letters as hard as she could. The next thing she knew, her eye beams were burning a big hole in the chart.

EMHSR
FTU20Z
SPPG1
ATSHW
RYZAB
V9WLMF

"Ooops!" Bubbles said. "Sorry!"

Dr. Wick smiled and marked her clipboard. "Eyesight and eye beams, check!"

"I'm going to test your reflexes, Buttercup," Dr. Cratson said. "Have a seat right over here, please."

Buttercup sat down on a bench.

Dr. Cratson took out a small rubber mallet. "Cross your right leg over your left leg, please."

Buttercup crossed her legs. Dr. Cratson tapped at her knee with the mallet.

WHAM! Buttercup's leg went flying out in front of her, kicking Dr. Cratson right in the chest. He went flying backward through the air and landed on top of a table full of test tubes.

Dr. Cratson stood up and brushed himself off. "Reflexes, check!" he said,

marking his clipboard.

Dr. Wick hurried over. "I think it's safe to say the Girls are in excellent health as usual," she said. She offered a jar of lollipops to the Girls.

"Thanks, Dr. Cratson. Thanks, Dr. Wick. See you next year!" the Girls called.

Blossom turned to her sisters. "I sure hope we didn't miss too much at school this morning."

Oh, don't worry, Blossom. I'm sure you didn't . . . or did you?

Chapter 2

When the Girls arrived at Pokey Oaks Kindergarten, they found the rest of their classmates outside for recess.

"Where were you guys?" Mitch Mitchelson asked the Girls. "Boy, you really missed all the action!"

"What do you mean?" Buttercup demanded. "What happened?"

"Don't pay any attention to him," Blossom said knowingly to her sisters. "He's just trying to make us feel bad." She turned to Mitch. "It just so happens that we had to have our yearly checkup. Besides, we didn't miss anything, and you know it!"

"Did so!" Mitch said. He called to the twins, Lloyd and Floyd Floijoidson. "Guys, The Powerpuff Girls missed all the action this morning, didn't they?"

Lloyd and Floyd nodded.

"It was terrible," Lloyd said.

Julie Bean and Robin Schneider wandered over. Mary Thompson and Harry Pit joined the group as well.

"This mean woman burst into our classroom and started spraying all this pink stuff all over the place," Julie said.

"Everyone was saying, 'Where are The Powerpuff Girls?!'" Mary reported.

"That's terrible!" Blossom said. "Who was this woman?"

"Some lady." Mitch shrugged. "She had long blond hair."

"And she was wearing a mask and a white jumpsuit," Robin volunteered.

"That sounds like Femme Fatale!" Blossom said.

"But why would Femme Fatale want to spray pink stuff all over everyone?" Bubbles asked.

That's a good question! Femme Fatale is known for beating up men and stealing Susan B. Anthony coins! Why would she care about the kids at Pokey Oaks?

"I can't believe it!" Buttercup

grumbled. "The one time something cool happens in school, and we're not here to see it."

"I hope no one got hurt," Bubbles said.

Mary shook her head. "Nobody even got a scratch."

"Thanks to Ms. Keane," Julie said proudly.

"The pink spray was headed right for us," Lloyd said.

"So Ms. Keane threw herself in front of all of us to protect us," Floyd said.

"She was covered in the stuff!" Mitch said.

"But not one drop got on any of the kids," Mary reported.

"Wow," Blossom said. "It sounds like Ms. Keane did an excellent job!"

"I still can't believe we missed all the

fun," Buttercup grumbled.

"Let's go inside and make sure Ms. Keane's all right," Blossom said.

The Girls flew across the yard and into school. They found Ms. Keane sitting at her desk, working on some papers. There were a few small traces of pink powder in her hair and on her clothes.

"Hi, Ms. Keane!" Bubbles sang out.

Ms. Keane looked up from her desk.

But wait, what's this? Is Ms. Keane actually . . . frowning?!

"Yes, Girls, what is it?" Ms. Keane asked gruffly.

"We heard about what you did this morning, Ms. Keane," Blossom said. "And we wanted to thank you for covering for us while we were gone."

"Where were you Girls, anyway?" Ms. Keane asked. Her cheeks were flushed

pink. "You're more than two hours late for school."

"We have a note from the Professor," Blossom explained.

"Okay, fine," Ms. Keane grumbled. "Now, go back outside, all of you. Recess isn't over for ten minutes."

Wait a minute! This doesn't sound like the usual cheerful, patient Ms. Keane we all know and love!

"Yes, Ms. Keane." The Girls glided toward the classroom door.

"What's her problem?" Buttercup muttered.

"Maybe she's just tired out from being a hero today," Blossom said.

As the Girls flew past the hamster cage, Bubbles stopped and pointed. "Hey, look!" she said. "Twiggy and Hammy got

sprayed, too! Oh, I hope they're all right!"
Sure enough, the class pets both had
traces of pink powder in their brown fur.

"They seem fine," Blossom said,
observing the hamsters. "Although
Twiggy sure is biting the bars of her cage
awfully hard."

"Girls!" Ms. Keane's
voice came at
them sharply from
across the room.
"I thought I told
you to go outside!"
"Yes, Ms. Keane,"
the Girls said again, zooming quickly
toward the door.

*Whew! That Ms. Keane's in some mood!
Well, maybe not everybody's cut out to be a
superhero. . . .*

chapter 3

The next day!

"I hope Ms. Keane feels better today," Bubbles said as the Girls flew to school.

"I bet all she needed was a good night's sleep," Blossom said.

"Either that or a major attitude adjustment," Buttercup grumbled.

The Girls zoomed into the classroom.

The moment they were inside, a mean voice barked at them. "Sit down! You're late again!"

The Girls turned and saw Ms. Keane standing by her desk. She wore an angry scowl, and now her whole face looked pink — much pinker than yesterday.

"But Ms. Keane," Bubbles objected.

"We're not late!" Buttercup insisted.

Blossom looked at the clock on the wall. "School doesn't start till —"

"School starts when I say it does," Ms. Keane snapped. "Now sit down."

The Girls looked around the room. The kids who were already there were sitting quietly at their desks. Everybody looked scared.

"But what about Free Play Time?" Bubbles asked meekly.

"Free Play Time?" Ms. Keane laughed meanly. "Forget it! This is *school*! There will be no more *playing* here!"

Blossom raised her hand. "Actually, Ms. Keane, recent educational studies show that young children such as ourselves learn very effectively through self-directed play and interacting with our peers."

"Can it, Blossom," Ms. Keane said.

Blossom was shocked. Ms. Keane had never, ever told her to "can it" before.

"Okay, everybody take out a piece of paper," Ms. Keane instructed. "I want you all to practice writing the letter *F*."

The children all got busy writing. Ms. Keane paced around the room, looking over the students' shoulders. Her face was getting pinker and pinker.

She stopped behind Floyd. "You call

this an F?!" she shrieked, snatching his paper. "This looks like a half-dead tree branch."

"I—I'm s-sorry, Ms. Keane," Floyd stammered.

"*You* of all people had better learn to make a proper F, Floyd," Ms. Keane said, her voice rising. Her cheeks were bright red. "If you don't learn to make an F, you'll never learn to write your name, and if you don't learn to write your name, you'll never be able to fill out a job application. And if you can't fill out a job application, you'll never be able to get a job! And without a job, you won't be able to feed or clothe yourself, AND YOU'LL BE ALONE AND HUNGRY FOREVER!!"

"Ms. Keane, I'm sure Floyd is trying

his best," Bubbles said sweetly. "And you always tell us that as long as we try our very best —"

"Well, his best just isn't good enough, then!" Ms. Keane barked. "And nobody asked you, Bubbles!"

Bubbles couldn't believe it. Ms. Keane had never spoken to her like that before.

"I'd like to give her an answer or two she hasn't asked for," Buttercup muttered, eyeing the teacher.

Mitch let out a laugh.

"Mitch Mitchelson!" Ms. Keane snapped. "Keep quiet!"

"It wasn't my fault!" Mitch objected. He pointed at Buttercup. "She —"

"And stop blaming others!" Ms. Keane shouted.

"But —" Mitch tried to protest.

"And stop being difficult!" Ms. Keane yelled. "In fact, I want you to write it out on a piece of paper for me — *'I will keep quiet in class and stop blaming others and being difficult.'*"

"All that?" Mitch asked in amazement.

"Ten thousand times," Ms. Keane instructed.

Mitch's mouth dropped open.

"Don't worry," Buttercup whispered. "My sisters and I will use our superspeed to help you write it."

"What's that, Buttercup?" Ms. Keane said, her face as red as a tomato. "Looks like you need a little lesson, too. No recess for you today!"

Buttercup was stunned. Ms. Keane had never taken away her recess time before!

Ms. Keane glared at the class. "In fact," she added, her face growing pinker, "no recess for anyone!"

Bubbles and Buttercup exchanged shocked looks. But Blossom watched her teacher with suspicion. Could it be a coincidence that Ms. Keane was behaving so strangely right after Femme Fatale's attack? She'd have to keep an eye on her. . . .

Later that day . . . while the kids of Pokey Oaks were maintaining complete silence as they practiced their letters . . .

there was a commotion from the hamster cage.

"Hey, look at Twiggy!" Bubbles said.

"Not the dumb hamsters again!" Buttercup sighed.

"No, look, she's pink," Bubbles said.

The Girls peered at the hamster cage.

Sure enough, Twiggy's fur was pink. She was running in her hamster wheel at a furious pace, creating a terrible racket.

"I guess that pink spray stuff really got to her," Buttercup commented.

"But then why isn't Hammy turning pink?" Blossom asked. "After all, he got sprayed, too."

Hammy was his usual brown furry self. As the Girls watched, Hammy approached the hamster wheel. As soon as he got close, Twiggy tried to bite him.

Hammy turned and ran. He hid deep inside an empty toilet paper roll in the far corner of the cage.

"So how come Hammy's still brown?" Buttercup wondered. "They're the same kind of hamster, right?"

Bubbles giggled.

"Well, not exactly," she said. "Twiggy's a girl, and Hammy's a boy."

"That's it!" Blossom shouted. "Whatever was in that pink spray probably only affects girls! That's why Ms. Keane and Twiggy are both pink, but Hammy is still brown. I'll bet Femme Fatale designed that spray to make girls tougher! She was going to spray it on the whole class so she could create a whole army of tough girls, but Ms. Keane ended up with a megadose!"

Good thinking, Blossom!

"Poor Ms. Keane," Bubbles said softly. "That pink spray made you too tough for your own good!"

"If it's tough girls Femme Fatale's looking for, she can stop looking right now," Buttercup said, practicing a few tae kwon do moves. "Come on, let's go get her!"

"Wait," Blossom said. "I have an idea — a plan to show Femme Fatale how tough the girls of Pokey Oaks can really be!" She huddled up with her sisters.

Go, Girls, go!

chapter 4

Later that day . . .

Blossom, Bubbles, and Buttercup zoomed down Main Street with the kindergarten girls marching in formation right behind them.

Buttercup called out, keeping time for the marchers. "Hup, two, three, four. Hup, two, three, four."

The rest of the girls sang out as they marched.

"We don't need no pink spray,

We'll fight anything in our way!"

"Hup, two, three, four. Hup, two, three, four."

"This way!" Blossom called, turning left on Main Street. "We won't give up till we've found her!"

"Look! There she is!" Bubbles yelled.

Femme Fatale froze when she saw the army of girls with Blossom, Bubbles, and Buttercup hovering overhead.

"That's right, Femme Fatale!" Blossom yelled. "Your dream has come true!"

"And your worst nightmare, too!" Buttercup added.

"Come on, Girls, let's get her!" Blossom called.

The army of girls sprang into action. Julie jumped in the air, delivering a tae kwon do kick just the way Buttercup had taught her. The kick sent Femme Fatale flying straight toward Blossom. Blossom socked Femme Fatale in the gut, and the villain went flying back the other way.

"Use your jump rope!" Bubbles called to Mary. "Just like I showed you!"

Mary sent out a jump-rope lasso. The loop of the lasso caught Femme Fatale

around the waist. Mary passed the end of the rope to Bubbles, who started swinging it around in a big circle. Femme Fatale flew around in the air.

Buttercup zoomed up to Femme Fatale and launched into a series of punches. Femme Fatale flew out of the lasso and landed on the ground.

"Come on, Robin," Blossom called. "Let's try that gymnast attack we practiced."

Blossom and Robin launched into a series of cartwheels. Their feet sliced into Femme Fatale, sending her spinning.

Finally, Femme Fatale was nothing more than a quivering lump. She looked up at them, her eyes pleading.

"Okay, okay, enough," she begged. "I give in. You win."

The Pokey Oaks girls broke into a cheer.

Blossom turned to her classmates. "You girls were great!" she said.

"You did it just the way we showed you," Buttercup added proudly.

Femme Fatale sniffed.

"Hey, what's that I see?" Blossom said, peering down into Femme Fatale's face. "Is that a tear?"

"You're not *crying*, are you?" Buttercup taunted. "I thought you were so tough!"

"Just think happy thoughts," Bubbles suggested. *"Think about a happy day, and then your tears will go away!"* she recited.

"Bubbles!" Buttercup yelled. "We just beat her up! We *want* her to be upset, remember?"

"Actually, what we want is for her to tell us how to cure Ms. Keane," Blossom said. She glared at Femme Fatale. "Our teacher got a megadose of that pink spray of yours, and she's turning really mean."

"She doesn't let us put the pretty stickers on the weather chart anymore or bring in stuffed animals for show-and-tell or anything," Bubbles explained.

"Tell us how to turn her back," Buttercup said. "Now!"

"Yeah!" the rest of the Pokey Oaks girls cried. "Change Ms. Keane back!"

Femme Fatale's head drooped. "There is no antidote," she said in a low voice.

"What?" Blossom said.

"There's no cure," Femme Fatale explained. "I never expected to want to reverse the process, to make anyone *less* tough."

Bubbles gasped. "You mean Ms. Keane is stuck being mean?"

Oh, no! Say it isn't so! Is Ms. Keane going to be Ms. Meane forever?

chapter 5

The next day!

Oh, no, look at Ms. Keane today! She's so pink now that she's actually red!

"Snack time!" Ms. Keane yelled.

The children rushed to their seats.

Ms. Keane passed out the snacks — stale bread crusts and lukewarm water.

The children looked down at their snacks, then back up at Ms. Keane's terrible red face.

35

"Eat!" Ms. Keane commanded. "You have ten seconds!"

The next day!
Yikes! Ms. Keane is redder than ever! Her eyes are wild, angry, and bloodshot! And she seems to be growing! What's going on here?!

The children were sitting at their desks, staring silently ahead.

"I HEAR SOMEONE!" Ms. Keane growled.

The children sat up straighter. Everyone tried to be as quiet as possible.

"I STILL HEAR SOMEONE!" Ms. Keane yelled. "SOMEONE IS DEFINITELY BREATHING!"

The next day!
Oh, no! Ms. Keane is turning into some

kind of magenta monster! She's huge! She's horrible! Aaah! Don't look!

Ms. Keane stomped angrily through the classroom, kicking blocks out of her way. The room shook with every step. Books, blocks, paints, and other school supplies were flying off the classroom shelves.

Blossom zoomed over just in time to catch a block that was about to hit Julie.

Bubbles saw a clay model fall off a shelf right above Harry. She quickly swooped down and lifted Harry out of the way to safety.

Buttercup spotted a book heading straight for Lloyd's head. She flew over and grabbed it before it hit him.

Ms. Keane let out an angry roar and knocked everything off her desk to the floor.

"This is nuts," Buttercup said to her sisters. "I say we beat up Ms. Keane."

Blossom gasped. "Buttercup! I know she's acting bad, but we can't beat up the teacher!"

"Besides," Bubbles added, "Ms. Keane is the bestest teacher ever. I know she's still good inside."

I don't know about that, Bubbles. I've heard of strict teachers, but this is getting ridiculous!

Later that night!

The Girls and the Professor were sitting together at the dinner table.

"So, Girls," the Professor said, serving himself some peas, "how was school today?"

"Terrible!" Buttercup burst out. "Ms. Keane is the meanest teacher ever!"

"Well, Buttercup, just about all teachers seem mean sometimes, when they don't do things the way we would like," the Professor said.

"Seriously, Professor," Blossom said. "There's something wrong with Ms. Keane. You see —"

"I know the feeling well," the Professor cut in with a chuckle. "Why, I remember my old teacher Mrs. Bain." He shook his head. "In our eyes, Mrs. Bain didn't do anything right. She used to make us take our spelling tests again and again until we got every single word right."

"Is that it?" Buttercup said. "No kicking blocks or lobbing lumps of clay? No three-hour nap times? No cleaning the toilets? No emptying out the sandbox one grain at a time?"

"Ms. Keane never made us do that with the sandbox!" Bubbles pointed out.

"It's on her list for tomorrow," Blossom said with a sigh. "I saw it, too."

"Well, I'm sure whatever she has planned for you, she's got a good reason," the Professor said kindly. "Now, if you Girls don't mind, I think I'll go into the living room and read my paper for a while."

"Good reason, huh? I'd like to give her a good reason for not bothering us ever again!" Buttercup said once the Professor was gone.

"Buttercup, we can't fight Ms. Keane!" Blossom reminded her. "It isn't her fault that she's acting this way. We have to come up with another solution."

"I think we should be patient with Ms.

Keane," Bubbles said. "After all, she's always been patient with us. Buttercup, remember when you were having trouble learning to tell time? Ms. Keane gave you all that extra-special help."

"That's true," Buttercup admitted.

"And Blossom, remember when everyone had to give a report about an animal, and you decided to do yours about bees?" Bubbles asked.

Blossom nodded. "It was called 'Evolutionary Changes in the North African Honeybee,'" she remembered.

"Well, Ms. Keane was the only one patient enough to sit through your whole report," Bubbles reminded her.

"Yeah, she stayed three hours after school looking at my maps and graphs," Blossom said. "You're right, Bubbles. But still, we have to do something. We can't just let Ms. Keane go on like this."

"Look!" Bubbles said excitedly. She picked up a piece of the *Townsville Times* that the Professor had accidentally left behind. "This is perfect!"

Bubbles showed her sisters the headline. It read:

TOWNSVILLE TIMES ANNOUNCES TEACHER OF THE YEAR CONTEST

"Let's enter Ms. Keane in the contest," Bubbles said.

"Teacher of the Year?" Buttercup said. "Are you kidding? Monster of the Moment is more like it!"

"But maybe she'll remember the kind of teacher she used to be," Bubbles said.

"It just might work," Blossom said. "Anyway, it's worth a try. Come on, let's see what we have to do."

Go, Girls, go!

The Girls got to work on their contest entry. Each Girl decided to make something special to convince the contest judges that Ms. Keane deserved to win.

When the Girls were all done, they decided to show the Professor what they had done. They zoomed into the living room.

"Professor, we had a great idea," Blossom said.

"Well, it was really my idea," Bubbles said.

"But I said I thought it could work," Blossom pointed out. "Buttercup was the one who didn't want to do it."

"Hey, I did my part!" Buttercup objected.

"Girls!" the Professor said. "Please, just stop arguing and tell me the idea."

"We're entering Ms. Keane in the Teacher of the Year Contest!" Blossom said.

"Because she's the bestest teacher ever!" Bubbles added.

"But mostly so she'll stop being so mean," Buttercup said.

"I used the computer to create my entry," Blossom said. "These charts and graphs mathematically document the specific ways that Ms. Keane has helped to improve her students' lives, and chart the exact impact of her effect on each student."

"That's impressive work, Blossom," the Professor said, looking at the charts.

"This is my entry," Bubbles said, holding up a big piece of paper. "It's a picture of a beautiful queen. I call her Queen Keane, because Ms. Keane is like a queen to me. And I made lots of flowers and rainbows and butterflies and hearts all around her. And I wrote a poem on the back. It goes like this:

"Ms. Keane is the bestest, she teaches us our letters.

Ms. Keane is the wonderfulest, she teaches us our numbers.

Ms. Keane is the sweetest, she tells us right from wrong, and right from left, too!

Ms. Keane is the specialest, terrificest, great-
est, nicest teacher ever!"

"That doesn't even rhyme," Buttercup
said.

"It doesn't have to!" Bubbles told her.
"Ms. Keane says a poem doesn't have to
rhyme — the most important thing is the
feeling in it. And my poem is full of feeling!"

"I think it's a lovely poem, Bubbles,"
the Professor said. "Now, Buttercup, why
don't you show me what you did?"

"Here." Buttercup thrust a piece of
paper at the Professor.

The Professor read it out loud. "'Ms.
Keane used to be OK. She taught me to tell
time.' Well, that's very — down to earth,
Buttercup. Well done, all of you."

"I hope it works," Blossom said.

"I hope Ms. Keane wins," Bubbles added.

"I just hope she stops kicking blocks around and leaves us alone," Buttercup put in.

Let's hope so, Girls!

chapter 7

A week later . . .

Blossom, Bubbles, and Buttercup stared at the newspaper in front of them. The headline read:

MS. DARLENE DARLIN NAMED
TOWNSVILLE TIMES
TEACHER OF THE YEAR!

Underneath the headline was a photo of a woman with dark hair and glasses, surrounded by a group of smiling kids.

"I can't believe it!" Blossom said.

Bubbles's eyes were filled with tears. "Ms. Keane didn't win!"

Buttercup scowled. "What a waste of time! Now we're stuck with a monster teacher forever!"

"How could they pick someone else instead of Ms. Keane?" Bubbles wondered.

Blossom picked up the newspaper. "It says here that Ms. Darlin won because she gave up her own pay for a whole year in order to take her class on a field trip to Japan. Then, since they had missed so many regular lessons while they were in Japan, she volunteered to come to each student's home during her vacation time to give them individualized special help." Blossom put down the paper in disgust. "What a show-off. Boy, some people just don't know when to stop!"

"I still think Ms. Keane is the bestest teacher ever," Bubbles said.

Ring, ring!

What's that? The Powerpuff hotline? No, it's the regular telephone. Better get it, Girls!

Blossom flew over to answer the phone. "Hello?" she said. "Yes, this is Blossom. . . . Yes . . . Who? . . . Yes, we did. . . . Really? . . . That's great! . . . Tomorrow? . . . We'll be there!"

Blossom zoomed back to her sisters. "That was the *Townsville Times* calling," she said. "It's about the Teacher of the Year Contest. Ms. Keane is a runner-up!"

"Big deal," Buttercup said. "I'd like to run *her* up — or rather, run her *out* — of town, that is!"

"They want to come to school tomorrow to take her picture with us," Blossom explained. "And they want us to present our contest entries to her then, too."

"That's great!" Bubbles said. "Now Ms. Keane will see that even though she didn't win the contest, she's still a winner to us!"

What a nice thought, Bubbles. I'm sure Ms. Keane will really appreciate — Aaah! What's that huge red angry monster doing at Pokey Oaks?

Wait a minute! Is that Ms. Keane? Is that huge ferocious red beast really the Pokey Oaks

Kindergarten teacher we all know and love? It can't be! But it is! It is!

The next day . . .

The children were involved in their morning activity — scraping gum off the bottoms of the desks. Ms. Keane stood at the front of the room, her huge red hands on her huge red hips. She glared at the children as they worked.

Then there was a knock on the classroom door. The door opened and a perky blond woman with a pad and pencil walked in. Behind her was a man wearing a camera around his neck.

The woman walked straight over to

Ms. Keane. "Howdy do? You must be Ms. Keane. I'm Doris Dane, reporter for the *Townsville Times.* I'm pleased to let you know that you've been selected as a runner-up in our Teacher of the Year Contest!"

"*Rrrrrr . . .*" Ms. Keane growled.

"Yes, well . . ." Doris Dane said. "We're here to take your picture with the students who entered you in the contest. Powerpuff Girls, are you here?"

Blossom, Bubbles, and Buttercup came out from under the desks they were scraping.

"Super. I'd like to get some shots of you Girls presenting your contest entries to Ms. Keane," Doris Dane said. She tugged on Ms. Keane's arm. "Come right over here, dear, please, right in front of the chalkboard, that's nice."

"Rrrrrr," Ms. Keane said as Doris Dane pulled her.

"Lovely," Doris Dane said. "Now, let's have you Girls line up alongside your teacher. . . . That's great." Next she handed Buttercup the contest entry Buttercup had made. "Go ahead, dear, read it out loud."

Buttercup looked down at the paper in front of her. "'Ms. Keane used to be OK. She taught me to tell time,'" she read quickly.

The camera was flashing. Ms. Keane stopped growling and looked at Buttercup.

"Super," Doris Dane said. She handed Blossom the charts Blossom had made. "You're next, dear."

Blossom cleared her throat. "Well, I've compiled a set of charts and graphs. This one here shows how many new things the class has learned with Ms. Keane. I've divided them into subsets to represent standard academic subjects such as mathematics and language arts, as well as areas of social development such as turn-taking and sharing with others. This next one shows . . ." Blossom went on, explaining the charts and graphs.

Hey, look! Look at Ms. Keane! She's stopped growling and she's even a little paler shade of red! What's happening?

"Terrific," Doris Dane said as the photographer continued snapping pictures. She handed Bubbles her picture and poem. "Your turn, dear."

Bubbles held up her picture and

smiled a big smile. "This is a picture of Queen Keane," she said. "It's really a picture of Ms. Keane, but I decided to make her a queen because I think she's the bestest teacher in the world, and I think she should have really won this contest, and you guys are mean not to make her the winner because she's the bestest teacher in the whole wide world, although I do appreciate that you made her a runner-up."

Hey, look at that! Ms. Keane's getting paler! Why, she's positively pink! And she's shrinking, too!

"Anyway," Bubbles continued, "I made lots of flowers and rainbows and hearts all around her because I love her so much! And I wrote her a poem, too, and here it is." Bubbles began to read.

By the time Bubbles had finished, Ms. Keane looked like her regular self again. She was her normal size, and all that was left of her pink color was a proud, happy glow on her cheeks.

"Oh, Bubbles!" Ms. Keane said. "Oh, Girls! That was wonderful! Thank you so much!" Ms. Keane bent down to hug the Girls.

The children climbed out from under the desks and began to cheer as the flashbulbs popped around them.

"Okay, I have what I need," Doris Dane said. "It'll be in tomorrow's paper. Thanks, everyone! Good-bye!" She and the photographer left.

Ms. Keane looked around at all the children. "I feel so much better now," she said. "I just haven't felt like myself lately. I don't know what it is, but it all started that day when that awful woman came in here with that pink spray."

"We knew the real Ms. Keane was in there somewhere," Bubbles said happily.

And so, once again, the day was saved, thanks to The Powerpuff Girls . . .

. . . oh, except as far as Hammy's concerned, but that's a matter he'll have to take up with Twiggy!